# SALTY SEAGULL

# HAPPY READING!

This book is especially for:

CAMERON

Suzanne Tate
3/17/96

Suzanne Tate,
Author—
brings fun and
facts to us in her
Nature Series.

James Melvin,
Illustrator—
brings joyous life
to Suzanne Tate's
characters.

For more information,
please call or write:
Nags Head Art
P.O. Box 88
Nags Head, NC 27959
(919) 441-7480

# SALTY SEAGULL

## A Tale of an Old Salt

Suzanne Tate
Illustrated by James Melvin

Nags Head Art
Number 12 of Suzanne Tate's Nature Series

*For Charlotte Truitt*
*my beloved teacher*
*—in honor of her 100th birthday!*

Library of Congress Catalog Card Number 92-60375
ISBN 1-878405-06-3
Published by
Nags Head Art, P.O. Box 88, Nags Head, NC 27959

Printed in the United States of America

Salty Seagull was a salty Old Salt.
He was wise in ways around the water.

Salty lived on Little Island with a big flock of gulls.
He was the oldest of his flock.

Salty's wings drooped down,
but they still carried him far.
And the feathers on them
were bright and black.

Salty proudly held his white head high.
Young birds in the flock—Cindy and Simon Seagull—
thought that he was the smartest gull of all.

But other gulls didn't think so.
When Salty tried to tell them
what they should or shouldn't do—
those gulls sassed him!

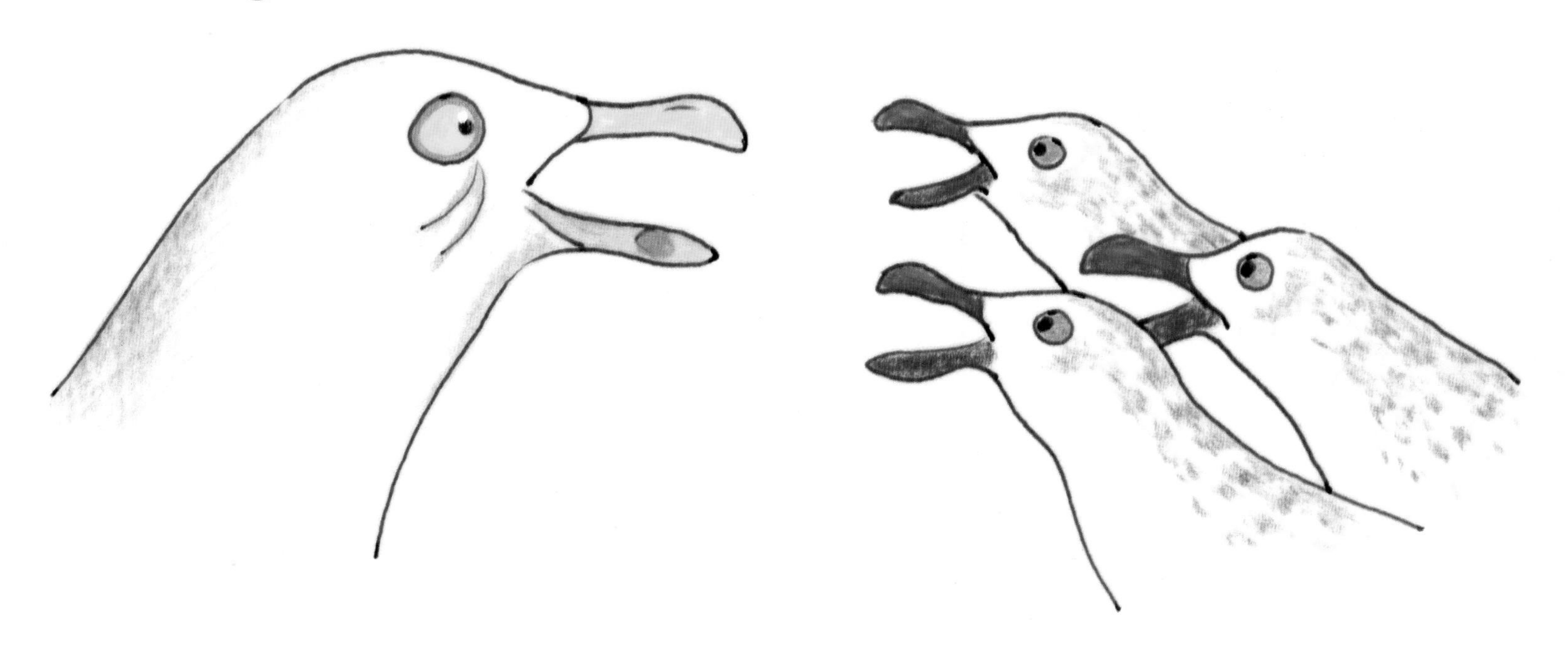

"Don't get your feathers ruffled,"
the sassy birds said to Salty.
(They really didn't think that he was very smart.)

In the summertime, all the gulls
led lovely lives on Little Island.
The weather was breezy and warm.
And there were lots of little fish for them
to catch and eat.

But one summer, a big rain came.
The wind picked up and blew and blew— it was blustery!
It blew so hard that the gulls
didn't even try to fly.

They huddled together on the ground
beside some bushes.
The gulls were afraid that they would blow away!

"Salty, what are we going to do?" cried Cindy Seagull.
She was scared!
"What's happening?" asked Simon Seagull,
trying to be brave.

"This is a 'hairy-cane,'" Salty said.
"I have seen many bad storms like this."

"Stay down and be still!" he said.
"We will soon see the eye of the storm.
The wind will stop blowing, and the sun will shine."

"Don't pay any attention to him!"
the sassy gulls said.
"Salty's just a bird-brained, old bird."

Then, the sassy gulls tried to fly.
But the wind carried them faster and faster.
It tumbled and turned them!

Suddenly, bright sunshine came out.
And the wind stopped blowing.
The weather was beautiful, just as Salty had said!
It was the eye of the hurricane.

Cindy Seagull soared into the sky.
She felt as free as a bird!
"Oh, how beautiful," she thought.
Simon Seagull flew up to join her.
"Salty was right," he said.

But Salty Seagull shouted,
"The storm will return!
Come back where it is safe."

So they all flew to the ground and
huddled together again.
The storm returned, as Salty said.
It blew and rained some more.
And then the storm was over.

The sassy gulls came straggling back to Little Island.
Cindy Seagull tried to tell them
about the eye of the hurricane.
But those sassy gulls shook their heads.
"Just some more of Salty's tales!" they said.

The season of hurricanes soon ended.
And the weather turned cold.
There were fewer and fewer fish in the waters
around Little Island.

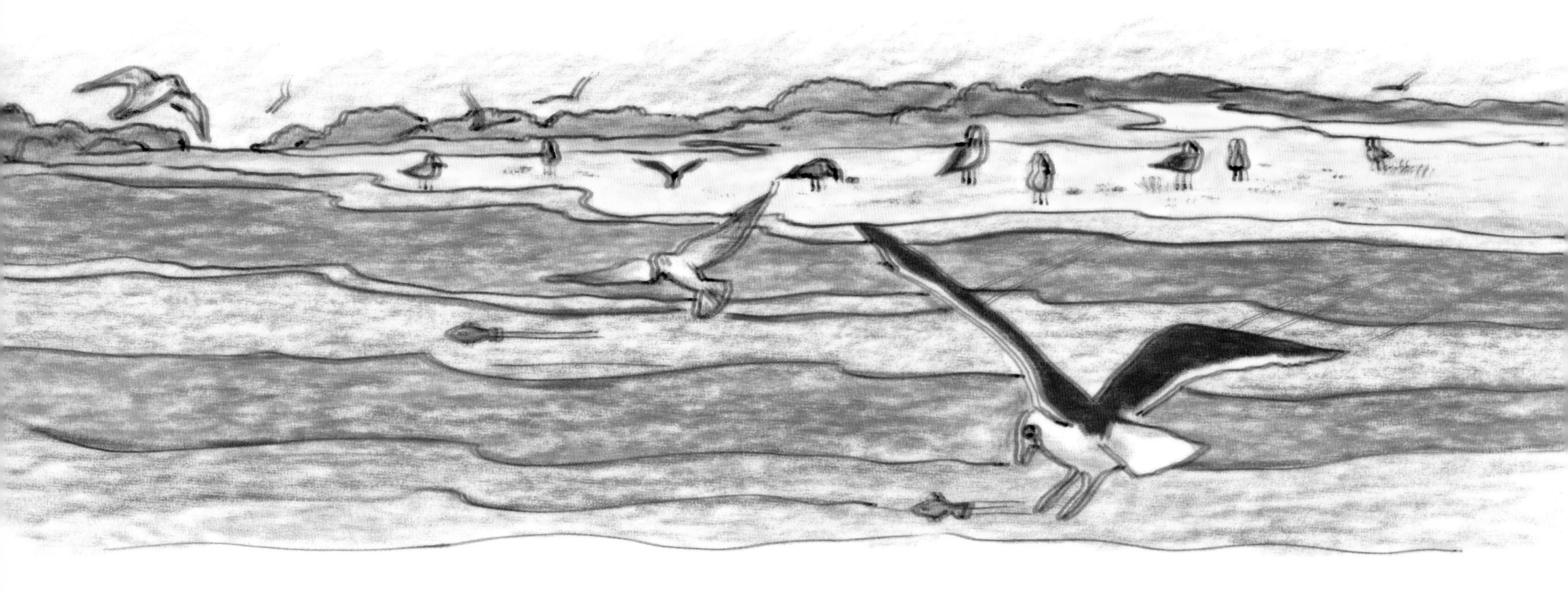

The gulls were having trouble
finding enough to eat.
They were getting hungry.

"What are we going to do for food?"
Cindy Seagull asked.
"Let's ask Salty," replied Simon Seagull.
"Maybe he has a plan."

Salty did know what they should do!
"We can eat clams," he said.

The sassy gulls laughed.
"What a bird-brained idea!" they cackled.
"You know we can't eat clams.
Their shells are too hard."

Salty Seagull didn't say another word.
He flew away over the water.
The other gulls watched as Salty dived
into the cold water.
Soon, he came up with a clam in his beak.

Then, he did a surprising thing!
Salty Seagull flew with the clam
to a nearby road.
He flew high above the road.

He dropped the clam, and its shell broke into pieces.
Juicy meat spilled out of it!

All the gulls were so surprised!
They, too, began diving and picking up clams
and dropping them onto the road.

The clams broke open, and meat spilled out.
The gulls had plenty of food to eat!

There was just one thing wrong.
When the gulls sat down in the road
to eat clams—CARS came along.
It was dangerous to eat clams on the road.

"Watch out for CARS!" Salty warned them.
And all of the gulls listened to him.

One day HUMANS came and worked near the road.
They were paving a parking lot
in front of a store.
The parking lot was black and hard.

Salty Seagull was pleased.
"What a good place to drop clams," he said.
"It should be a safer place for us."

As soon as the parking lot was done,
the gulls began to drop clams on it.

"You were right, Salty," said Cindy Seagull.
"The parking lot is safer than the road.
The store is closed this time of year—
we won't have to worry about CARS."

None of the gulls was ever again sassy to Salty.

...the gulls said as they all dropped clams. And thanks to Salty Seagull—they never went hungry in the wintertime again!